NANCY DREW

#25

AND THE CLUE CREW®

Buggy Breakout

WITHDRAWN

BY CAROLYN KEENE

ILLUSTRATED BY MACKY PAMINTUAN

Aladdin

New York London Toronto Sydney

🪔 ALADDIN
An imprint of Simon & Schuster Children's Publishing Division
1230 Avenue of the Americas, New York, NY 10020
First Aladdin paperback edition March 2010
Text copyright © 2010 by Simon & Schuster, Inc.
Illustrations copyright © 2010 by Macky Pamintuan
All rights reserved, including the right of reproduction in whole or in part in any form.
ALADDIN is a trademark of Simon & Schuster, Inc., and related logo is a registered trademark of Simon & Schuster, Inc.
NANCY DREW and related logos are registered trademarks of Simon & Schuster, Inc.
NANCY DREW AND THE CLUE CREW is a registered trademark of Simon & Schuster, Inc.
For information about special discounts for bulk purchases, please contact Simon & Schuster Special Sales at 1-866-506-1949 or business@simonandschuster.com.
The Simon & Schuster Speakers Bureau can bring authors to your live event. For more information or to book an event contact the Simon & Schuster Speakers Bureau at 1-866-248-3049 or visit our website at www.simonspeakers.com.
Designed by Lisa Vega
The text of this book was set in ITC Stone Informal.
Manufactured in the United States of America
10 9 8 7
Library of Congress Control Number 2009927035
ISBN 978-1-4169-7814-5
ISBN 978-1-4169-9899-0 (eBook)
0116 OFF

CONTENTS

CHAPTER ONE

Bug Week

"I love Bug Week!" Nancy Drew said, doing a little skip as she walked down the hall toward class.

"Me too!" her friend George Fayne piped up.

"Me three!" Bess Marvin added. "Check out my cool bug outfit!" She twirled around, showing off the red ladybugs on her white T-shirt. The pockets of her jeans were embroidered with different-colored butterflies.

Nancy giggled. Leave it to Bess to come up with a fashion statement about bugs. Bess was way into clothes. George, Bess's cousin, was more into sports.

This week was Bug Week for the third graders

at River Heights Elementary School. The girls' teacher, Mrs. Ramirez, was teaching the students all about insects.

The day before, they had watched a cool movie about common bugs and their habitats, or homes. Today they were going to make bug posters, and tomorrow they were going on a field trip to the new River Heights Insectarium. Nancy couldn't wait!

The three girls walked into the classroom and took their seats. The rest of the students were already sitting down. Up front, Mrs. Ramirez was writing some words on the blackboard:

HEAD
THORAX
ABDOMEN

The teacher turned around. "Can anyone tell me what's so important about these three things?"

A boy named Michael Dorf waved his hand

back and forth. "Mrs. R.! Mrs. R.! Mrs. R.!"

"Yes, Michael D.?" Mrs. Ramirez said. She called him that because there was another Michael in the class: Michael Lawrence, or Michael L.

Michael D. sat up very straight. "All insects have a head, a thorax, and an abdomen. What is a thorax? A thorax is the part of the body between the head and the abdomen." He spoke precisely, like a scientist.

"Very good, Michael D.," said Mrs. Ramirez. "Can anyone tell me what—"

"Insects have other things in common too," Michael D. interrupted. "Like three pairs of jointed legs, two antennas, compound eyes, and a hard exoskeleton. What are compound eyes? Compound eyes are eyes that are made up of lots and lots of simple eyes. With compound eyes, insects can look in many different directions at the same time. What is an exoskeleton? An exoskeleton is a skeleton that's on the outside of the body instead of the inside. Like a turtle's shell."

Nancy stared at Michael D., impressed. He sure knew a ton of stuff about bugs!

"Very good, Michael D.," Mrs. Ramirez said. "Can anyone tell me if spiders are insects?" Michael D.'s hand flew into the air. "Someone other than Michael D., that is," she added.

Luna Valeri raised her hand. "Um . . . they're insects? I hate them because they're creepy-crawly and supergross."

"Hmm. They're definitely creepy-crawly. But *are* they insects? Anyone else?" Mrs. Ramirez peered around the room.

Sonia Susi put her hand up. "Actually, they're not insects. They don't have antennas. And they don't have compound eyes." She turned to Luna. "I'm kind of scared of them too," she said with a grin.

"That's right, Sonia," said Mrs. Ramirez. "All right, class. I'm going to pass out some poster board and markers. We're going to make posters of our favorite, or not-so-favorite, bugs. First you will pick a bug to be your subject. Then you're going to draw your bug and label its head, thorax, and abdomen. You will label its other parts too, like its antennas, eyes, and wings—that is, if your insect has wings. Who can name an insect that has wings?"

Michael D. raised his hand again. So did Nancy. "Nancy?" Mrs. Ramirez said, pointing.

"Bees," replied Nancy.

Michael D. leaned across the aisle. "You forgot wasps," he whispered. "And butterflies. And moths. And dragonflies. And—"

"She said *an* insect," Nancy whispered back.

"Very good, Nancy," said Mrs. Ramirez. "While I pass out the supplies for your posters, why don't you all start thinking about what bug you'd like to draw?"

"Can I draw Bess Marvin?" Michael L. joked.

Bess whirled around and glared at him.

"Michael L., that's enough," Mrs. Ramirez warned him. "Also, class? Don't forget that tomorrow is our field trip to the River Heights Insectarium. Anyone who hasn't given me their permission slips, I need them now."

Sonia raised her hand. "Mrs. Ramirez? Can I make an announcement about something bug-related?"

"Yes, of course, Sonia," Mrs. Ramirez replied.

Sonia stood up and brushed her long, wavy blond hair out of her face. "I wanted to tell everybody about the River Heights Elementary School Bug Club," she began. "We're accepting new members! We meet once a week, and we share stories about our pet bugs. We already have three members: Michael D., Michael L., and me. I'm the president."

Nancy glanced over her shoulder at Michael L. He was bent over his notebook, doodling something that looked like a big, fire-breathing

dragon. He wasn't paying the slightest bit of attention to Sonia's announcement. Nancy was surprised that he was a member of the Bug Club. He didn't seem that interested in bugs. Yesterday, during the bug movie, he had gabbed with Antonio Elefano the whole time and gotten in big trouble with Mrs. Ramirez.

"We're going to be starting a website about bugs soon," Sonia went on. "And this Thursday, we'll be bringing our pet bugs to school for Bug Show-and-Tell, and—"

But Sonia was interrupted by an angry voice. "Stop the Bug Club!" someone shouted. "It's got to be shut down—now!"

ChAPTER TWO

Scorpion Attack!

Nancy craned her neck to see who had interrupted Sonia. It was Carly Henek. She wore a black T-shirt that said FREE THE BUGS!

Sonia put her hands on her hips. "Why are you telling people to shut down my club, Carly? That's so mean!"

Carly stood up and put her hands on her hips too. "*I'm* not mean.

You know what's mean? Keeping bugs in cages as pets . . . *that's* mean. So is the Insectarium. They keep bugs in cages too."

"I appreciate where you're coming from, Carly," Mrs. Ramirez told her. "It's great that you're worried about how the bugs are treated. But I think the members of the Bug Club take good care of their bugs. The people who work at the Insectarium take good care of their bugs too. In fact, bugs in captivity probably do better than bugs in the natural world. After all, bugs in nature have to deal with predators attacking them and eating them."

Michael D. raised his hand. "Mrs. R. is right! In the natural world, bugs have to fight off birds, amphibians, small mammals, fish, spiders, and even other bugs. Edgar is much safer in his cage at home."

"Edgar? Who's Edgar?" George spoke up.

"Edgar is my pet hissing cockroach," said Michael D. proudly. "You'll all be meeting him on Thursday during Bug Show-and-Tell."

"H-hissing c-cockroach?" Bess whispered to Nancy.

Nancy shrugged. She wasn't sure she wanted to meet something called a "hissing cockroach" either.

"I still think keeping bugs in cages is wrong," Carly insisted. She held up something that looked like a flier, printed on light green paper.

"Anyone who wants to join my club should talk to me during lunch or recess. I can give you a flier. Free the bugs!" she exclaimed, then sat back down.

Sonia sat down too. Nancy glanced back and forth between Sonia and Carly. *Wow, Bug Week is getting really interesting!* she thought.

"Welcome to the River Heights Insectarium," Mr. Valeri said. "Who here has ever been to an insectarium before?"

A few kids raised their hands. "I've been to the one in Montreal," Kevin Garcia said.

"I've been to the one in Philadelphia," said Nadine Nardo.

"I've been to both of them," Deirdre Shannon bragged. Deirdre was always bragging about something.

Luna Valeri raised her hand. "I've been to *this* insectarium before because you're my dad," she said.

Mr. Valeri looked embarrassed. "Uh, right. So, boys and girls! As you'll see, we have both mounted displays and live displays, in vivariums. Does anyone here know what a vivarium is?"

Michael D. raised his hand. "A vivarium is

kind of like an aquarium. It's a place where you can raise live animals, such as insects, under natural conditions." Next to him, Michael L. rolled his eyes.

"Are the bugs in the mounted displays . . . um, dead?" Bess asked nervously.

"Yes, they are. In fact, some of them are more than a hundred years old," Mr. Valeri replied. "In addition to the insects in our vivariums and in our mounted displays, we also have a live butterfly and moth room. We'll stop by there later this morning. You'll be able to walk around an enclosed space while butterflies and moths from all over the world fly around your head." He started walking toward a wide, arched doorway. "But first, we're going to visit the mounted display room. Please follow me. Take your time looking at the displays, and feel free to ask me any questions."

"This place is awesome!" George said as everyone headed into the mounted display room.

There were dozens of glass cases filled with all sorts of insects.

Nancy noticed that Carly wasn't looking at the glass cases but was instead passing out fliers to some of the other kids. She was wearing another "Free The Bugs!" T-shirt today, this time in purple.

"This place is *super*awesome!" Sonia agreed. "I wish I had my camera!"

"Do you like to take pictures of bugs?" Nancy asked Sonia.

Sonia nodded. "I love, love, love taking pictures of bugs! Especially my pet bug! Let me show you." She reached into her book bag and pulled out a photo. "Isn't she beautiful?" she said proudly.

Nancy, George, and Bess gathered around to look at the picture. Sonia's bug had a shiny black shell that reminded Nancy of patent leather dress-up shoes. It was posing next to a silver teaspoon and a mug with Sonia's name on it.

"What kind of bug is it?" asked George.

"It's a bess beetle," Sonia replied.

"A . . . what?" Bess said, looking startled.

"A bess beetle. Hey, Bess, they named a bug after you!" Sonia joked. "Isn't that cool?"

Bess frowned. "I'm . . . not sure."

"She's got a cool name, too. Princess Bess," Sonia added.

Bess's face lit up. "Princess Bess? That *is* a cool name."

"My, what a fine bess beetle specimen!"

Nancy turned around. Mr. Valeri was standing behind her, peering over her shoulder at Sonia's photo.

"Her name is Princess Bess," Sonia told Mr. Valeri.

"Oh, so she's yours? She looks quite large next to that spoon," Mr. Valeri observed.

"She's almost two inches long," said Sonia. "I measured her last week."

"My! That's very large," Mr. Valeri remarked. "In fact, that's one of the largest bess beetle specimens *I've* ever heard of."

"Really?" said Sonia eagerly.

Luna walked up to the group and tugged on Mr. Valeri's sleeve. "Dad? I need to talk to you," she whispered.

"Just a second, Luna. Can't you see I'm busy?" Mr. Valeri said impatiently. He turned back to Sonia. "Yes, indeed! I'll have to double-check, but your Princess Bess might hold some sort of record."

Sonia gasped. "Oh my gosh! Wait'll I tell the other members of the Bug Club!"

Just then there was a loud scream. It came from Michael D. "Scorpion!" he yelled. "I'm being attacked by a scorpion!"

CHAPTER THREE

Bug Show-and-Tell

Michael D. was jumping up and down in the doorway and tugging on his T-shirt. "Scorpion!" he shouted. "He put a scorpion down my back!"

He pointed to Michael L., who was standing a few feet away from him. Michael L. was laughing so hard that his shoulders were shaking.

Both Mrs. Ramirez and Mr. Valeri rushed up to Michael D.

The other third graders, including Nancy, circled around the Michaels to see what was going on.

A second later, a wriggly-looking scorpion fell out of Michael D.'s T-shirt and tumbled to the floor. Several kids screamed.

Nancy bent down to take a closer look. The scorpion was small and brown and shiny. *Too* shiny. She had seen pictures of scorpions. They were shiny, but not *this* shiny.

"It's not real," Nancy announced. "It's fake!"

"What?" Michael D. stopped jumping up and down and stared at the scorpion. He turned to Michael L., his face red and angry. "You tricked me! How dare you!"

"You fell for it, Dorf the Dork." Michael L. smirked. "Guess you're not such a bug expert, huh?"

"I know *way* more about bugs than you!" Michael D. shot back.

Mrs. Ramirez held up her hands. "Boys! Enough! Michael L., I want a word with you—now!"

Michael L. stopped smirking and followed Mrs. Ramirez out of the room. Michael D. picked the fake scorpion off the floor and stuffed it into his pocket hastily. Nancy thought he looked kind of embarrassed.

"I guess I'll wait to tell the other Bug Club members about Princess Bess," said Sonia with a heavy sigh. "Especially since the other Bug Club members hate each other."

"I don't think they hate each other," Nancy reassured her. "They're just having a dumb boy fight. They'll get over it."

"This is Edgar," Michael D. said. "He's a hissing cockroach. Hissing cockroaches are also called Madagascar hissing beetles. They are related to common cockroaches, but they're nothing like them. For one thing, they're very clean. For another thing, they don't have wings. They originally came from Madagascar, which is an island off the coast of Africa. You can tell that Edgar is a boy because girls have smooth antennas, and boys have hairy antennas. See?"

Everyone gathered around Michael D.'s desk and studied Edgar, who was perched on top of his small white cage. He was about two inches long, with a pill-shaped body that was black and brown. He had long, thin antennas with tiny hairs on them.

"Can you pick him up?" Antonio asked Michael D. "Does he bite?"

"Yes, you can pick him up. And no, he doesn't bite." Michael D. reached down and scooped Edgar up in his hand. Edgar hissed, then crawled quickly up Michael D.'s arm.

"Ew!" several kids cried out, backing up.

"No, no, he's harmless," said Michael D.

"I think Edgar would be a lot happier living in Madagascar, where he belongs," Carly said pointedly. Today, her "Free the Bugs!" T-shirt was sky blue.

"Edgar didn't come from Madagascar," Michael D. explained. "He came from Elio's Exotic Pets, downtown."

Carly rolled her eyes. "Whatever."

Everyone moved on to Sonia's desk next. Her bug was perched on top of a small green cage. The cage had holes but no windows, so it was hard to see inside.

"This is Princess Bess," said Sonia. "She's a bess beetle. Bess beetles have really strong teeth, because they like to chew wood. When they're upset, or when they want to talk to other bess beetles, they make a squeaky sound by rubbing their wings together."

Nancy stepped forward to check Princess Bess out up close. She looked exactly like she did in her picture. Nancy noticed a few other details, though—like her big, fierce teeth and also some subtle golden fringe along her legs and the edges of her body.

The class gathered around Michael L.'s desk next. Nancy noticed that his bug was still inside its cage, which was brown.

"And *this* is the coolest bug in the entire Bug Club," Michael L. announced. "His name is

Dragon Breath. Dragon Breath is an assassin bug. Assassin bugs are super dangerous. That's why Dragon Breath had to stay in his cage. He bites! And he eats other bugs. His favorite food is cockroaches!"

He grinned meanly at Michael D. as he said this last part. Michael D. glared at him and quickly returned Edgar to his cage.

"That's great. Thank you, members of the Bug Club!" said Mrs. Ramirez brightly. "Now we're going to be looking at—"

"No, no, we're not done yet!" Sonia interrupted. "We have another Bug Club member. Luna joined us yesterday. She has a bug to share too!"

"Oh! Wonderful!" Mrs. Ramirez smiled expectantly at Luna.

Luna reached into her bookbag and pulled out a small green cage. It was the same kind of cage as Sonia's. She set it down on her desk and opened the cage door, and a long, light brown and green bug scurried out. "This is, um, my pet praying mantle," she explained.

Mrs. Ramirez frowned. "You mean . . . praying *mantis*?"

Luna nodded. "Yes! That's what I meant! This is my praying mantis!"

She fell silent. She reached up and twirled her curly red hair.

"So . . . what does your praying mantis eat?" Mrs. Ramirez prompted Luna.

"Um . . . food?" said Luna.

"I think they like to eat other bugs too," Michael D. offered. "They'll also eat tiny little pieces of raw meat."

"Ew," Madison Foley said.

"What's his name?" George spoke up.

"Um . . . Praying Mantis?" said Luna hesitantly.

"Lame," Michael L. muttered under his breath.

As Nancy checked out Praying Mantis, she wondered why Luna had joined the Bug Club. She seemed even less interested in bugs than Michael L.!

After lunch and recess, everyone went back to the classroom so they could continue with Bug Show-and-Tell. Mrs. Ramirez had told the students to come up with three observations about each bug.

"Observations like, 'Princess Bess has a really cute name'?" Bess said to Nancy and George as they headed to their desks.

Nancy and George laughed. "Or maybe,

'Princess Bess has really scary fangs, like a vampire,'" George joked.

Bess made a face. "Ha ha."

"Oh, no!"

Nancy turned around. Sonia was standing next to her desk, and she looked really upset.

"What's wrong, Sonia?" Nancy asked her.

"It's Princess Bess. She's gone!" Sonia cried.

CHAPTER FOUR

Bugs on the Loose

"What do you mean, Princess Bess is gone?" Nancy asked Sonia.

Sonia pointed to her pet beetle's green cage. "The door's open. And she's not inside!"

"Maybe she crawled out," George suggested.

"How could that happen? I closed the door before lunch. I latched it too. I'm sure of it!" Sonia bent down and peered all around her desk. "Here, Princess Bess! Where are you, Princess Bess?"

Mrs. Ramirez came up to the girls. "What's going on?"

Sonia explained quickly. Mrs. Ramirez listened, then cupped her hands over her mouth.

"Boys and girls," she called out. "Sonia's pet beetle is missing. Please stay right where you are and don't move an inch. Princess Bess might be crawling around on the floor, and I don't want her getting stepped on. Very carefully, look all around you. Let me know right away if you see her."

Everyone started buzzing and whispering. Nancy did as Mrs. Ramirez said, searching for Princess Bess without moving her feet. She didn't see any sign of the beetle.

However, she did see something else . . . something small and crumpled up right next to Princess Bess's cage. She picked it up and smoothed it out on the palm of her hand. It was a sticker of a black beetle, and it kind of looked like Princess Bess.

Nancy wondered if it

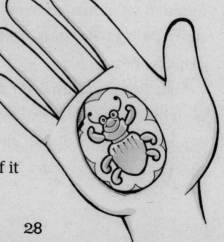

belonged to Sonia—or someone else. She put it in her pocket, thinking that it might be a clue.

Nancy loved finding clues. She, George, and Bess belonged to a club of their own, called the Clue Crew. The Clue Crew solved mysteries, everything from tracking down missing chicks to catching an April Fools' Day prankster. Whenever they were on a case, they looked for clues and kept track of them, both in Nancy's special purple detective notebook and on her computer at home.

"Hey, I found a bug!" exclaimed George suddenly.

"Is it Princess Bess?" Sonia asked her eagerly.

"Um . . . no. It's . . . it's a praying mantis," George replied after a moment. She reached down on the floor and picked it up very gingerly. "Is this your praying mantis, Luna?"

"I'm not sure." Luna squinted at the insect in George's hand. "They all kind of look the same to me."

"Is Praying Mantis still in his cage?" Bess

asked Luna. "That's the easiest way to figure it out."

Luna peered into the small green cage on her desk, opening the door a crack. "Um . . . no. So I guess that *is* Praying Mantis. Thanks for finding him, George!"

"You're welcome. Here, do you want me to put him back in his cage?" George offered.

"No! He escaped before, so maybe there's something wrong with the cage. Like maybe it's broken? I brought this other thing with me . . . let's put him in there." Luna reached into her bookbag and pulled out a plastic container. The lid had half a dozen holes for air. She took Praying Mantis from George and placed him

inside the container. Then she tucked both the cage and the plastic container in her bookbag.

"Maybe *my* cage is broken too," Sonia said worriedly. "Maybe that's how Princess Bess got out." She ran her fingers over the cage door, checking for problems. "Hmm, I don't know. It *seems* okay."

Everyone continued searching for Princess Bess. Mrs. Ramirez said it was okay for people to move around, as long as they were careful and kept their eyes on the floor. But Princess Bess was nowhere to be found. She didn't seem to be anywhere in the classroom.

At one point a thought occurred to Nancy. What if someone had deliberately set the Bug Club members' insects loose? That would mean Edgar and Dragon Breath might be missing too.

"Hey, Michael D.? Michael L.? Are *your* bugs still in their cages?" Nancy called out to the boys.

The Michaels checked their respective cages. "Edgar's right here," Michael D. replied after a moment. "And Dragon Breath is here," Michael L. added.

Nancy frowned. This meant that someone had set Princess Bess and Praying Mantis loose, but not Edgar and Dragon Breath. Or the first two bugs had gotten out by accident, but not the other two.

"What do you think happened to Princess Bess?" George asked Nancy and Bess quietly.

"I don't know, but we've got to find her!" said Bess, pouting.

Sonia approached the three girls. "Can I ask you something?" she whispered. "You guys have some sort of club, right? A detective club?"

"The Clue Crew," Nancy replied. "Why?"

Sonia glanced over her shoulder. She nodded in the direction of Carly, who was sitting at her desk and scribbling in a notebook. *"She's* the one who set Princess Bess free," she declared firmly. "Can you guys arrest her and get my beetle back?"

Chapter Five

Elio's Exotic Pets

"Why do you think Carly took Princess Bess?" Nancy asked Sonia. She and the other girls spoke in low voices so that no one else would overhear.

"It's so obvious! She's the president of the Free the Bugs! Club. That's why she set Princess Bess free," Sonia replied.

"Do you have any proof?" said George.

Sonia looked confused. "What do I need that for?"

"Did you see her do it?" Bess added.

Sonia shook her head. "No."

Nancy, George, and Bess exchanged glances. "We'll take your case and help you find Princess

Bess," Nancy told Sonia. "And we'll definitely put Carly on the suspect list. But we can't just accuse her of taking Princess Bess without any proof."

"Oh." Sonia made a face. "Okay, I guess," she said after a moment. "Thanks for taking my case! I hope you guys find Princess Bess fast. She's my favorite pet in the whole world!"

"So do you think Carly took Princess Bess?" George asked Nancy.

It was after school, and the three friends were heading outside with their bookbags. They all lived close to school, so they were allowed to walk home by themselves.

"I'm not sure," Nancy replied. She spotted Carly hurrying toward one of the school buses parked at the curb. "There she is. Maybe we should talk to her?"

"I have a better idea. Let's trick her!" Bess suggested.

"What do you mean, Bess?" said Nancy.

"Watch." Bess ran up to Carly. "Hey, Carly?"

Carly stopped in her tracks. "Yeah?"

"Do you have those Free the Bugs! fliers with you?" Bess asked her in a friendly voice. "Can I have one? I'm really, really interested in what you're doing."

Carly's face lit up. "Yeah? I didn't know you were interested. Here, wait a sec."

She bent down to open up her bookbag. Bess bent down too and peeked inside.

Nancy guessed what Bess had meant by tricking Carly. Bess was pretending to be interested in the fliers so she could see if Princess Bess was in Carly's bookbag—maybe in a cage or container.

Nancy craned her head over Bess's shoulder, trying to get a look inside Carly's bookbag too. She saw some books and notebooks and other stuff—but no cage or container or anything else that might be used for smuggling bugs.

Carly fished out one of her fliers and handed it to Bess. She handed a couple to Nancy and George, too.

Nancy scanned it quickly. Printed on light green paper, the flier read:

FREE THE BUGS!

Would YOU want to be kept in a cage as a pet or a museum display?

Well, neither do bugs!

 Return bugs to their natural habitats!

(That means OUTSIDE!)

Join the FREE THE BUGS! Club today!

There were bug stickers all over the flier: ladybugs, bees, butterflies, and more.

Nancy glanced over at Bess and George's fliers. They had some of the same stickers, but some different ones too.

Nancy reached into her jeans pocket, feeling for the crumpled-up beetle sticker she had found next to Princess Bess's cage. Sonia had told her earlier that the sticker didn't belong to her.

Could that sticker have come from one of Carly's fliers?

Did that mean Carly really *was* the one who had set Princess Bess free?

"I'm going to have a double scoop of Silly Strawberry," Nancy said.

"I'll have a double scoop of Mango Madness," said George.

"Hmm, these flavors *all* sound good. I can't decide," Bess said, scanning the menu.

"Maybe you should have one of each," George said. "That would be a *lot* of ice cream!"

The three girls were sitting in a booth at I Scream for Ice Cream, a new ice cream parlor in downtown River Heights. Hannah Gruen, the Drews' housekeeper, had brought the girls there as a special treat.

Nancy loved Hannah, who was a lot more than a housekeeper. Hannah had helped raise Nancy since she was three years old, when Nancy's mother died. She was kind and smart and funny. She brushed Nancy's hair every night. *And* she made the yummiest cupcakes in the world.

"Well, I think I'm going to have a raspberry sorbet smoothie," Hannah said, setting her menu down on the table. "So girls, how was school today?"

"The Clue Crew got a new mystery to solve," Nancy told her excitedly.

"It's about a missing bug," added George.

"It's not just any bug. Her name is Princess Bess!" Bess piped up.

Hannah's eyes widened as she glanced from

one girl to the other. "A new mystery? A missing bug? Princess Bess? My gosh! Tell me everything!"

The waitress came by to take their orders. After she left, Nancy and her friends filled Hannah in on their case.

"Do you have any suspects yet?" Hannah asked when the girls were finished.

Nancy nodded. "We have one suspect. Carly Henek."

"She has this club called Free the Bugs!" Bess explained. "I think she might be the only member so far . . . but whatever. It's still a club."

"And Nancy found a bug sticker next to Princess Bess's cage," George went on. "Carly's Free the Bugs! fliers have stickers all over them."

"That's a pretty interesting clue," Hannah remarked. "Did you record it in your notebook yet, Nancy?"

"Not yet. Thanks for reminding me!" Nancy reached into her bookbag and pulled out her special detective notebook. Her father had given it to her a long time ago so she could keep track of her cases. She also took out her favorite purple pen.

Nancy opened the notebook to a clean page. She wrote:

THE CASE OF THE MISSING BESS BEETLE

SUSPECTS
Carly Henek. She thinks bugs shouldn't live in cages.

CLUES
A sticker of a beetle. It kind of looks like Princess Bess. It was right next to Princess Bess's cage. Maybe it belongs to Carly? Her "Free the Bugs!" fliers have bug stickers on them.

Nancy thought about something else. Princess Bess was missing. And Luna's pet bug, Praying Mantis, had *almost* gone missing. Had the bug-napper—whoever it was—been after both bugs? If so, why those two and not Edgar or Dragon Breath?

"Hey, is that Michael L.?" Bess said suddenly.

Nancy glanced up from her notebook. Bess was staring out the window next to their booth.

Bess was right. Michael L. was walking into a shop across the street, carrying something small and square under his arm.

Something small and square . . . like a bug cage?

Nancy squinted, trying to read the sign above the door. It said ELIO'S EXOTIC PETS.

Nancy frowned. She remembered Michael D. saying that he had bought his hissing cockroach, Edgar, there.

Then she remembered something else. Mr. Valeri had said that Princess Bess might be special and even some kind of record holder because she was so big.

Maybe Michael L. had stolen Princess Bess so he could sell her to the owner of Elio's Exotic Pets!

CHAPTER SIX

A New Suspect

Nancy told George, Bess, and Hannah about her suspicions. "What if he's going to sell Princess Bess?" she said worriedly.

"Michael L. is so mean. He *would* do something like that," Bess said.

"Let's go stop him!" said George, jumping to her feet.

Hannah told the waitress that they would be back in a few minutes for their ice cream. Then the four of them rushed out the door and went across the street to Elio's Exotic Pets.

The inside of Elio's was unlike any other store Nancy had ever seen. There were walls and walls of cages and aquariums with different kinds of animals. One wall had snakes, some of them curled up in a ball, others slithering along tree trunks and branches. They made Nancy shiver a little. Another wall had chameleons and geckos and even a creature called a "bearded dragon." Nancy had thought dragons only existed in myths and fairy tales!

Yet another wall had more familiar exotic pets, like turtles and frogs. Nancy especially liked one of the frogs, which had a green body, orange legs, and big, bulgy, reddish orange eyes.

"There he is!" whispered George. She pointed to a cluttered counter in the back of the store.
Michael L. was

talking to a man with curly brown hair and wire-rimmed glasses.

"Let's sneak up on him," Bess suggested. "That way, we can catch him . . . uh . . . red— red—"

"Red-handed?" Hannah suggested.

Bess nodded. "Yeah, that's it! Red-handed."

The three girls tiptoed down one of the side aisles so they could avoid being seen—or heard—by Michael L. Hannah followed at their heels. Along the way, they passed a wall full of spiders and insects. Nancy saw several hissing cockroaches and assassin bugs. She also saw some scorpions. She didn't see any bess beetles, though.

When they were a few feet away from the counter, Nancy stopped and put her finger up to her lips, to indicate that they should be silent.

"So I think there's something wrong with him," Michael L. was saying to the man with the glasses.

"Why?" the man asked.

"Well, he's not eating as much as he used to. And he's kind of cranky."

"What do you mean, cranky?"

Nancy noticed that Michael L. was saying "he." Princess Bess was a she. Did that mean he was talking about a different bug?

"Can I help you ladies?"

Nancy started. The man behind the counter was looking straight at her and her companions.

Michael L. whirled around. "What are *you* doing here?" he demanded.

"We . . . uh . . . we're thinking of getting some new pets," Nancy fibbed.

Michael L. narrowed his hazel eyes suspiciously. "Yeah? Like what kind?"

"I saw a cute little green snake back there!" Bess piped up.

"Yeah, and I *love* spiders," added George. "What about you, Nancy?"

"Maybe a frog, as long as it gets along with Chocolate Chip," Nancy improvised. Chocolate Chip was her little Labrador retriever puppy. "So what are *you* doing here?" she asked Michael L.

"Yeah! Who's in there?" Bess stepped forward to take a peek into Michael L.'s cage. "It's not a bess beetle, is it? Like a certain bess beetle named . . . *Princess Bess*?"

"What are you talking about? This is Dragon

Breath. He's sick!" Michael L. exclaimed. "I brought him here because he came from this store. I thought Mr. Elio could help me."

Nancy looked into the cage too. Inside was the same brown insect from the Bug Show-and-Tell presentation earlier that day. Michael L. was telling the truth.

"Why are you guys so interested in Princess Bess, anyway?" Michael L. said. "So she's gone. Big deal! Sonia should just get another one."

"How can you say that? Princess Bess is her pet! Plus, she's bigger and better than all the other bess beetles," Bess pointed out. "Princess Bess rules!"

"Whatever." Michael L. rolled his eyes.

"Do *you* know what happened to her?" Nancy asked him.

Michael L. shrugged. "Maybe."

George put her hands on her hips. "You'd better tell us!"

Michael L.'s lips curled up into a nasty smile. "Maybe Dragon Breath ate her. Maybe that's why he's feeling sick. Because he got a stomachache!"

"Ha ha, very funny," Bess retorted. *"Not!"*

"What happened to your bess beetle?" Mr. Elio asked Nancy.

"She's not mine. She belongs to our friend at school. And she's missing," Nancy explained.

"That's too bad. Well, if your friend wants a new one, I've got some bess beetles coming in next week," said Mr. Elio.

"Thanks, I'll let her know," Nancy said. She didn't add that Bess was right. Princess Bess was Sonia's pet. She probably wouldn't want to replace her with just any other bess beetle any more than Nancy would want to replace Chocolate Chip with another puppy.

Ten minutes later, back at I Scream for Ice

Cream, Nancy dug into her double scoop of Silly Strawberry and thought about Michael L. She remembered how he had put a fake scorpion down Michael D.'s back yesterday at the Insectarium. Michael L. obviously enjoyed playing pranks. He also liked making people mad, like when he said he wanted to draw Bess for his bug poster, or all the times he called Michael D. "Dorf the Dork."

She wondered, could Michael L. have stolen Princess Bess as a prank, or to make Sonia mad? Could he be a new candidate for their suspect list?

ChaPTER SEVEN

Another Buggy Clue

On Friday, Nancy was one of the first students to walk into Mrs. Ramirez's classroom. The only other student there was Michael D., and he was doing something really weird. He was placing a small log on the floor in the corner of the room. Peering around, Nancy saw that there were logs in the other three corners too.

"What are you doing?" Nancy asked him curiously. She wondered if she should add him to the suspect list along with Carly and Michael L.—just because he was acting so strangely!

Michael D. glanced up. "Oh! Hi, Nancy! Yes, well, I did some research last night, and I discovered that bess beetles are attracted to old,

rotting logs. So I had my parents call Mrs. Ramirez and ask her if it would be okay for me to bring a few logs to class today. As you can see, I have one in each corner of the room. If we're lucky, one of them will attract Princess Bess." He added, "That is, if she's still in this building."

"Oh." Nancy had never heard this fact about

bess beetles. She was impressed that Michael D. was going to the trouble of trying to lure Princess Bess.

I guess I won't put him on the suspect list just yet, she thought with a smile.

By lunchtime, Princess Bess hadn't made an appearance at any of Michael D.'s logs.

"Poor Princess Bess," said Bess, digging her fork into her mac and cheese but not taking a bite. "She's been missing for twenty-four whole hours. She's probably really, really hungry by now. And cold. And lonely."

She, Nancy, and George were sitting at a table at the far end of the cafeteria. Nancy was eating a tuna salad sandwich that Hannah had packed for her. George had peanut butter and jelly.

"If Princess Bess is hungry, she'll just eat a desk or something," George said. "Aren't our desks made of wood? She likes wood, right?"

"I think they're made of metal," Nancy piped

up. "I think she'd like one of Michael D.'s yucky logs better."

Carly walked by just then, carrying a tray. She was wearing another "Free the Bugs!" T-shirt, this time in yellow.

She stopped when she saw Nancy and her friends. "Hey! Are you guys still thinking about joining my club?" she asked in a friendly voice.

"Oh, yeah. We had some questions to ask you. Do you want to sit with us?" said Nancy. She had been waiting for a chance to talk to Carly some more, because she was one of the Clue Crew's top suspects.

"Sure!" Carly sat down in the empty chair across from Nancy. Nancy noticed that her plate was piled high with all sorts of veggies, like carrots and peas and string beans.

"I'm a vegan," Carly said, following Nancy's gaze.

"Is that like a vegetarian?" asked Bess curiously.

"Kind of, except that I don't eat any food that

comes from animals. That means I don't eat milk or butter or cheese or eggs or anything like that," Carly explained.

"One of my mom's best friends is a vegan," George said. "Whenever she comes over for dinner, my mom makes her this really yummy pasta dish with lots of veggies in it and no cheese."

"That's cool!" Carly smiled. "So . . . are you guys ready to become part of the Free the Bugs! movement?"

Nancy, George, and Bess exchanged glances. "We kind of wanted to know about your club first. Like, what do you do exactly?" Nancy asked Carly.

Carly popped a carrot into her mouth. "I talk to people about bugs and how they shouldn't live in cages. I pass out fliers. I'm putting a website together. Stuff like that."

"Do you . . . well, do you ever actually *free* bugs?" said Nancy.

Carly stared at her. "Uh, no."

"Why not? That's the name of your club, right? Free the Bugs!" George said.

"Yeah, but I can't just go around randomly setting bugs free," said Carly. "That would be just as mean as keeping them in cages. They have to be returned really carefully to their natural habitats. You know, by bug scientists or whatever. Otherwise they'd just get lost or sick or eaten by predators."

Nancy watched Carly carefully. She *seemed* to be telling the truth. On the other hand, she could be a good liar.

"So you didn't set Princess Bess free?" Bess said.

Carly glared at Bess. "Oh, so *that's* what this is about? You guys were just *pretending* to be interested in my club, weren't you? You're really just trying to snoop around about Princess Bess." She added, "For your information, I didn't set Princess Bess free. And I didn't steal her either." She stood up to go.

"Wait! We have proof against you!" Bess told her.

"Proof? What proof?" Carly demanded.

Nancy pulled the crumpled-up bug sticker out of her bookbag. She had been keeping it in there, in an envelope. "This. We found it next to Princess Bess's cage, right after she disappeared. It's from one of your fliers, right?"

Carly took a close look at the sticker. "Yeah, probably. But lots of people have my fliers, and all my fliers have bug stickers on them. Anyone could have peeled this sticker off one of the fliers. They peel off really easily. See?" She pulled one of her fliers out of her bookbag and started peeling off the bug stickers, one by one.

Nancy watched Carly. She was right. The stickers *did* peel off very easily.

Nancy wondered

if their suspect list had just grown to everyone in their class, based on the sticker clue.

At the end of the school day, everyone left Mrs. Ramirez's classroom and hurried into the hall to their cubbies. Nancy, George, and Bess lingered behind to check on Michael D.'s logs. The girls spread out into separate corners.

"Do you see Princess Bess?" Nancy called out to George and Bess.

"Nope, no Princess Bess," Bess replied. "There's an ant crawling around inside this one, though."

"And there's a fly on this one," said George.

Nancy peered closely at the log in her corner. She didn't see Princess Bess—or any other insect. She got up and inspected the log at the other end of the wall. She didn't see any bugs there, either.

She was about to get up when she saw something green poking out from beneath a nearby bookshelf. Curious, she reached for it.

It was a pocket folder—the kind used for

organizing notes and homework. *Someone must have left it there by accident,* Nancy thought. She opened it, wondering who it belonged to.

Inside was a single document, tucked into one of the pockets. The paper read, "The Care and Feeding of Bess Beetles." It included information about what they ate and what kind of habitat they required.

Nancy stared closely at the inside of the folder. There were a bunch of bug doodles and what looked like a hastily scribbled name: MICHAEL.

Chapter Eight

The Two Michaels

Nancy's thoughts raced to the second name on the Clue Crew's suspect list: Michael L.! The green folder was major proof against him. He must have stolen Princess Bess. And he must be keeping her at his house or elsewhere, using the instructions on the "Care and Feeding of Bess Beetles" sheet.

Nancy ran up to George and Bess and showed them the new clue.

"Michael L. is so busted!" Bess said angrily when Nancy was finished. "Let's go find him!"

"We'd better hurry. I think he rides the bus home," said George.

The three girls raced out of the room. They

found Michael L. at his cubby, dumping its contents on the floor and sorting through them carelessly.

"You stole Princess Bess!" Bess blurted out.

Michael L. glanced up. "Huh? What are you talking about, Bess Beetle?" he said impatiently.

"We found *this*," Nancy cut in. She held out the green folder for Michael L. to see.

Michael L. took it from Nancy and leafed through it. "This isn't mine," he said after a moment. "Besides, it says 'Michael,' not 'Michael L.' It probably belongs to Dorf the Dork. Why don't you ask *him* about it?"

Nancy started. It hadn't occurred to her that the folder might belong to Michael D. After all, he was a huge bug lover. He had even set out the yucky logs to try to lure Princess Bess out of hiding. There was no way he could be the bug-napper.

Could he?

Nancy and her friends said a quick good-bye to Michael L. and rushed off to find Michael D. He was outside, shuffling toward the line of school buses along with a bunch of other kids.

"Michael D.!" Nancy called out.

Michael D. stopped and turned around. He waved when he saw the girls. "Hi! How is your investigation going?" he said.

Nancy frowned. How did he know that she, George, and Bess were on a case? *The* case? On the other hand, Michael D. always seemed to know everything.

"Is this yours?" Nancy said, showing him the green folder.

Michael's eyes lit up. "Yes, it is! Thank you! I thought I'd lost it."

"Why do you have that thing in there about the care and feeding of bess beetles?" George asked him pointedly.

"Is it because you bug-napped Princess Bess? You're keeping

her prisoner in your house, aren't you?" Bess accused.

Nancy fixed her eyes on Michael D. "Well?"

Michael D.'s cheeks turned bright red. "I didn't bug-nap Princess Bess!" he exclaimed. "I would never do a thing like that. I printed out that sheet about bess beetles from the Internet so I could come up with ideas on how to find

Princess Bess. Like the idea about the rotting logs."

Nancy frowned. "Really?"

"Really. I'm already working on some new ideas," Michael D. went on. "I'm thinking of buying a bess beetle and setting her loose in the school, so the two beetles might communicate with each other." He added, "Of course, that will only work if Princess Bess is still here."

Michael D. seemed to be sincere. And he *had* been doing a lot to help Sonia find Princess Bess.

"I have to catch my bus," Michael D. said, glancing over his shoulder. "I have another idea, though. Why don't we all pay another visit to the Insectarium tomorrow? Mr. Valeri might have some valuable suggestions on how to find Princess Bess. After all, he *is* an expert on insects."

"Pass the chips, please," Bess said.

"Which kind? The nacho cheese, or the salsa blast?" Nancy asked her.

Bess giggled. "Hmm. How about both?"

Nancy, Bess, and George were hanging out in Nancy's room, chowing down on the snacks that Hannah had prepared for them. It was Friday night, and they were having a sleepover at the Drews' house.

George was sitting at Nancy's computer, going through the file on "The Case of the Missing Bess Beetle." As part of the Clue Crew, it was George's job to update the file on the computer.

"So far, we have two clues," George said as

she scrolled down the screen. "The beetle sticker. And the green folder."

"Michael D. had a good explanation about the green folder, though," Nancy pointed out.

Bess took a sip of her hot chocolate. "Yeah, but I still think he should be on the suspect list. He's really smart. That means he could be a good liar, too."

"Whipped cream mustache!" George pointed to Bess's face.

"What? Oh!" Bess wiped her mouth with the back of her pajama sleeve. "So if we include Michael D., how many suspects do we have?"

"Three. Carly, Michael L., and Michael D.," George replied.

"I still wonder why the bug-napper went after Princess Bess and Praying Mantis, but not Edgar and Dragon Breath," Nancy said thoughtfully. "Did the person want to steal those bugs for some reason, but not the other two? Or did they want to pull a prank on Sonia and Luna, but not the Michaels?"

"That's it!" said George suddenly. Her brown eyes were sparkling.

"What's it?" Bess asked her curiously.

"I know who the bug-napper is," George said excitedly. "Actually, bug-*nappers*, plural. It's Michael L. and Michael D.!"

ChaPTER NiNE

An Unexpected Twist

Nancy thought about George's new theory. Could the Michaels have been in cahoots to steal or free Princess Bess—and Praying Mantis, too?

"But they don't even like each other," Bess pointed out. "Michael L. calls Michael D. 'Dorf the Dork' all the time. And remember at the Insectarium, when he put that fake scorpion down Michael D.'s shirt?"

George mulled this over. "Maybe they're just pretending to hate each other," she guessed.

"Why?" said Bess.

"So they could bug-nap the two bugs and get away with it," George replied.

"I know!" Nancy said. "We're meeting Michael D. at the Insectarium tomorrow, right? We can talk to him some more and see if he says or does anything suspicious."

"Good idea," Bess said.

Nancy sipped her hot chocolate and gazed thoughtfully out her bedroom window. Maybe tomorrow would be their lucky day. Maybe tomorrow they would solve the mystery of Princess Bess's disappearance once and for all!

"Well, this is very disturbing about poor Princess Bess," Mr. Valeri said.

It was Saturday morning. A big group was gathered in the mounted display room of the Insectarium. In addition to Mr. Valeri, Nancy, George, Bess, Hannah, Michael D., and Michael D.'s dad were there. Sonia had come along too, with her mom and her little sister, Eden.

Luna was also there, hovering near her dad. She seemed uncomfortable and out of place, staring down at her shoes a lot. Which was weird, Nancy thought, since her dad was in charge of the Insectarium.

Nancy had just finished filling Mr. Valeri in about Princess Bess. "Do you think you can help us find her?" she asked him.

Mr. Valeri nodded thoughtfully. "Yes, I hope so. I have some detailed information about bess beetles on my computer. Let me go retrieve that now. I'll be back in a sec."

After he left, Nancy turned to Sonia. "I know you're worried about Princess Bess," she said. "I have a good feeling, though. I think we're really close to finding her!"

"I hope so," said Sonia.

"I have a pet bug too!" Sonia's sister, Eden, spoke up. She reached into her pocket and pulled out a stuffed ladybug toy. "See? She's weal!"

"What's her name?" Nancy asked her.

"Wadybug!" Eden giggled. "She's going to eat you! And you, too!" She thrust the ladybug at Luna, who was standing close by. Luna gave a little scream and jumped back.

"Sorry, my sister's a spaz," Sonia apologized to Luna. "Hey, how's Praying Mantis? And how's the cage working out?"

Luna looked startled. "Huh? What? Oh! Praying Mantis is fine. And the cage is fine too." She wandered away to study a display case full of fuzzy moths.

Nancy leaned over to Sonia. "Why did you ask Luna about her cage?" she whispered, so Luna wouldn't hear.

"Luna has the exact same kind of cage

as me," Sonia replied, also whispering. "She asked me what kind of cage I had. She said she wanted the same thing for her new bug."

"When did she ask you that?" said Nancy.

Sonia scrunched up her face. "Ummm . . . oh, yeah. It was on Wednesday. Right after our field trip. That's when she told me she wanted to join the Bug Club."

"Our field trip to . . . here?" asked Nancy.

Sonia nodded. "Luna was weird about it, though. I asked her what kind of pet bug she had. And she said something, like, 'You know. A regular bug.'" She paused. "It's like she didn't know what kind of bug she had or something. I mean, everyone knows what a praying mantis is, right?"

"Right." Nancy stared at Luna, who had moved on to a display case full of beetles. She was twirling a lock of her hair around her finger.

Why would Luna have wanted to get the exact same cage as Sonia? Nancy wondered. She tried

to remember the chain of events on Thursday, the day Princess Bess disappeared. Right after Sonia said Princess Bess was missing, George had found Praying Mantis on the floor. She had offered to put Praying Mantis back in his cage. But Luna had insisted that she herself put Praying Mantis in a separate container—a plastic container with holes.

Luna must have left school that day with the cage *and* the plastic container. Nancy remembered seeing her put both items into her bookbag.

Then a crazy thought occurred to her. What if Princess Bess had been in Praying Mantis's cage—or what everyone *thought* was Praying Mantis's cage? What if the cages had been switched?

What if Luna was the bug-napper?

ChaPTER TEN

Rescuing Princess Bess

Nancy thought about it some more. Luna had bought the exact same bug cage as Sonia. What if she simply switched cages right after Bug Show-and-Tell? She could have taken Praying Mantis out of his cage and set him down for a minute, which would explain why he had wandered off, only to be found by George a short time later.

Luna could have then switched cages, putting Praying Mantis's empty cage on Sonia's desk and taking the cage containing Princess Bess for herself. The identical green cages had holes but no windows, making it hard to see inside. It would have been easy to get away with the switch, especially if the other students were distracted or looking the other way.

The question was . . . why? Luna barely seemed interested in bugs. Why would she want to steal Princess Bess?

"I'll be back," Nancy said to Sonia. She grabbed George and Bess and pulled them aside. "Guess what? I think I figured it all out," she whispered.

"You mean about Michael L. and Michael D. being the bug-nappers?" George whispered.

Nancy shook her head. "No. I think Luna is the bug-napper!"

"What?" George and Bess said in unison.

Nancy told her friends about her theory. When she was finished, Bess nodded excitedly. "You're right. That makes sense! Luna *is* the bug-napper. Yay, Nancy, you've solved the mystery!"

"What do we do now?" George said.

"Now we talk to Luna." Nancy marched toward Luna, who was still staring moodily at the beetle display case. George and Bess followed.

Everyone else was spread around the room, checking out the other display cases and talking. Mr. Valeri still hadn't returned from his office. Nancy tapped Luna on the shoulder. "Hey, Luna? Can we talk?" she said.

Luna turned around. She blinked nervously at Nancy. "Uh . . . sure."

"We know you took Princess Bess," Bess burst out.

Luna's blue eyes widened. "W-what are you t-talking about?" she stammered.

"You set Praying Mantis loose, and then you switched cages with Sonia," George spoke up.

"W-why would I do something like th-that?" said Luna.

"I don't know. You tell us," Nancy said.

Luna opened her mouth, then closed it again. Her eyes welled up with tears. "Okay," she said after a moment. "I took Princess Bess. Just like you said. But it was all my dad's fault!"

"What do you mean?" Nancy asked her.

"My dad is only interested in bugs, bugs,

bugs! It's so stupid! I try to talk to him about stuff that *I'm* interested in, like books and soccer and movies. But he's not interested unless it's bug-related." Luna wiped her eyes. "I saw him looking at the picture of Princess Bess during the field trip on Wednesday. I thought that if I could, you know, get her for him somehow, he'd be impressed. So I came up with my plan. All I had to do was get a cage and a bug and join the Bug Club, so I could be part of Bug Show-and-Tell on Thursday. I bought the cage at a pet store— the same cage as Sonia's. And I found Praying Mantis in our garden." She added, "That beetle sticker you found was mine, Nancy. I saw you picking it up. It came from one of Carly's fliers. I thought that if I left it there, people would think Carly was the bug thief or something."

"You did all this because of me?"

Nancy and the others whirled around. Mr. Valeri was standing there, holding a pile of computer printouts. Nancy thought he looked sad and mad at the same time.

Luna started crying again. "I'm sorry, Daddy! I know what I did was wrong."

"So . . . where is Princess Bess now?" Mr. Valeri demanded.

"I brought her home to show her to you on Thursday night," Luna explained. "I was going to tell you that Sonia gave her to me as a present. But . . . but . . ." She hesitated.

"But what?" Nancy prompted her.

"But she got loose in my bedroom, and now I can't find her," Luna admitted. "I feel really awful! I have no idea where she is!"

Nancy stared across the room at Michael D., who was pointing to one of the display cases and talking animatedly to his dad. "I have an idea for how we can find her," she said finally.

"Shh, everyone!" Michael D. held his finger up to his lips.

He, Nancy, George, Bess, Sonia, and Luna were all sitting on the floor of Luna's bedroom. Hannah, Michael D.'s dad, Sonia's mom,

Sonia's little sister, Eden, and Mr. Valeri were hanging out in the living room downstairs. They had all been camped out at the Valeris' house for the last couple of hours, waiting for Princess Bess to make an appearance.

Luna's best guess was that Princess Bess was still somewhere in her room. She had been very careful about keeping her door shut for the past two days, since Thursday. *I hope she's right,* Nancy thought.

Earlier, Michael D. had set up several old, rotting logs in various spots around Luna's room. Mr. Valeri and the other grown-ups had helped carry the logs in from the backyard.

Nancy's gaze kept bouncing around the room, trying to catch the slightest movement. George and Bess were looking around carefully too and making hand signals to each other. Luna was fiddling nervously with her hair. So was Sonia.

Michael D. was leaning forward so far that his ear was practically touching the floor.

"What are you doing?" Sonia whispered to him.

Michael D. put his finger to his lips again. A moment later he said, "Did you guys hear that?"

"Hear what?" whispered Bess.

"Listen!" Michael D. said.

Everyone listened intently. Nancy heard a faint noise coming from one of the logs, which was in the corner closest to the window. It was kind of a squeak and kind of a lip-smacking sound too, like when people blew kisses at each other.

"That's a bess beetle noise!" said Michael D. excitedly.

He got on his knees and crawled over to the log. His eyes lit up, and he made a thumbs-up sign. "There she is!" he announced. "Princess Bess is here, safe and sound!"

Sonia crawled over to the log too. "Oh my

gosh, it's her!" she cried out. "Hey, Princess Bess! You're back! Remember me?"

Then Nancy, George, Bess, and Luna gathered around the log. Nancy recognized Princess Bess's shiny patent leather shell, big teeth, and golden fringe. The beetle was having an afternoon snack, nibbling on the rotting wood.

Sonia turned to Nancy, George, and Bess. "Thank you guys so much for finding Princess

Bess!" she gushed. "And thank you, too, Michael D.!"

"No problem at all," Michael D. replied. He grinned at Nancy. "Perhaps I should start my own detective club. I could specialize in finding missing bugs."

"Yeah. You could call your club the Critter Crew," George joked.

Everyone laughed.

Make Your Own Bug Habitat!

Nancy, George, and Bess loved observing bugs during Bug Week. You can observe bugs at home by building a simple bug habitat.

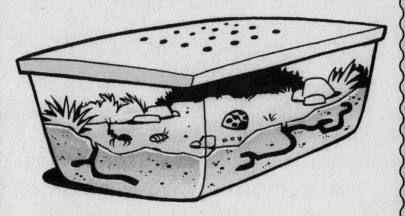

You Will Need:

A clear plastic produce container with holes. This is the kind of container that holds berries, tomatoes, herbs, salad mix, and other types of fruits and vegetables. Ask your parents to clean one of these containers for you after they're done with it.

Dirt, grass, leaves, sticks, and rocks from outside. You could also collect some moss, acorns, flowers, and whatever else you think a bug might like.

A few cotton balls

Something to capture your bug, like an insect net or clean cup

A bug!

A field guide to bugs from a bookstore or library, so you can identify different kinds of bugs, what they like to eat, and so forth. You could also get this information online on websites about bugs. Ask your parents to help.

Let's Get Started!

❀ Fill the plastic produce container with dirt, grass, leaves, sticks, and other things you collected. Think about making it look like a mini garden for your bug.

❀ Find a bug for your habitat. The best places to look for bugs are under rocks and bricks, under (and inside) logs, under loose bark on trees, and on plants. You might even find a bug inside your house, like an ant or a fly.

❀ Very carefully capture your bug and put it inside your habitat, then close the lid. Before capturing your bug, ask your parents (and check your field guide) to make sure it's not dangerous or poisonous.

❀ Soak a cotton ball in water and put it inside the habitat so your bug will have something to drink.

❀ Check your field guide (or a bug website) to learn all about your bug. Find out what it likes to eat, and make sure to feed it!

❀ Observe your bug for a few hours. Make notes about its behavior . . . draw pictures of it . . . even take pictures of it, if you have access to a camera.

❀ When you're done observing the bug, set it free where you found it.

OH . . . AND DON'T FORGET TO NAME YOUR NEW BUG BFF!